YES WE CAN!

A SALUTE TO CHILDREN
FROM PRESIDENT OBAMA'S VICTORY SPEECH

SCHOLASTIC INC.

New York   Toronto   London   Auckland   Sydney
Mexico City   New Delhi   Hong Kong   Buenos Aires

Photography credits for
Yes We Can! A Salute to Children from President Obama's Victory Speech
Cover: Barack Obama: Jason Reed/Reuters; Kids: Michael Frost; Flag: Tetra Images/SuperStock;
Back cover: Jason Reed/Reuters; Page 1: Flag: Tetra Images/SuperStock;
2: Bottom left: Michael Frost; Top left: Jason Reed/Reuters;
3: Jason Reed/Reuters; 4: Jim Young/Reuters; 5: Alex Brandon/AP Photo;
6: Patrick D. McDermott/UPI Photo/Newscom; 7: Jae C. Hong/AP Photo;
8: Top left: Chris Carlson/AP Photo; Bottom left: Bill Bachmann/Alamy;
Right: Copyright 2008 NBAE © Ron Hoskins/NBAE via Getty Images; 9: Wilfredo Lee/AP Photo;
10: Emmanuel Dunand/AFP/Getty Images; 11: Joe Raedle/Getty Images;
12: Jason Reed/Reuters; 13: Matt Sullivan/Reuters;
14: Ozier Muhammad/The New York Times/Redux;
15: Jim Young/Reuters; 16: Miles R. White/Scholastic; 17: Carlos Barria/Reuters;
18: Charles Ommanney/Getty Images;
19: Left: Emmanuel Dunand/AFP/Getty Images; Top right: Brian Snyder/Reuters;
Bottom right: Photodisc/Veer; 20: Riccardo Gangale/AP Photo; 21: Adi Weda/epa/Corbis;
22: J. Scott Applewhite/AP Photo; 23: Michael Francis McElroy/ZUMA Press; 24: Joshua Lott/Reuters;
25: Jim Young/Reuters; 26: Pat Benic/UPI/Landov; 27: Shannon Stapleton/Reuters;
28: Brian Kersey/UPI/Landov; 29: Jae. C. Hong/AP Photo; 30: Kuni Takahashi/MCT/Landov;
31: Pat Benic/UPI/Landov; 32: Jason Reed/Reuters

ISBN-13: 978-0-545-16366-8 / ISBN-10: 0-545-16366-8
Text copyright © 2008 from Barack Obama's Victory Speech (November 5, 2008)
Illustrations copyright © 2008 · All rights reserved.
Compilation copyright © 2009 Scholastic Inc.
Published by Scholastic Inc. SCHOLASTIC and associated logos are trademarks and/or
registered trademarks of Scholastic Inc.

10 9 8 7 6 5 4 3 2   09 10 11 12 13

"We are not enemies, but friends," per Abraham Lincoln's First Inaugural Address (March 4, 1861)

Book design by Whitney Lyle
Printed in the U.S.A.   40
First edition, January 2009

Change has come to America.

The road ahead will be long.

Our climb will be steep.

We as a people will get there.

I will be honest with you.

I will listen to you.

I will ask you to join in the work
of remaking this nation.

Block by block, brick by brick.

We are not enemies, but friends.

I need your help.

It cannot happen without you.

Yes, we can.

Yes, we can.

Yes, we can.

This is our moment.

This is our time....